To him who is able to do immeasurably more
than all we ask or imagine.

BLOOMSBURY CHILDREN'S BOOKS
Bloomsbury Publishing Inc., part of Bloomsbury Publishing Plc
1385 Broadway, New York, NY 10018

BLOOMSBURY, BLOOMSBURY CHILDREN'S BOOKS, and the Diana logo are trademarks of Bloomsbury Publishing Plc

First published in the United States of America in July 2021
by Bloomsbury Children's Books

Bloomsbury books may be purchased for business or promotional use. For information on bulk purchases please contact
Macmillan Corporate and Premium Sales Department at specialmarkets@macmillan.com

Library of Congress Cataloging-in-Publication Data
Names: Gilbert, Leah (Leah Rose), author.
Title: The perfect plan / by Leah Gilbert.
Description: New York : Bloomsbury Children's Books, 2021.
Summary: Maya plans to build the perfect treehouse, but after doing research and
selecting the perfect spot, she finds she must recruit helpers to get the job done.
Identifiers: LCCN 2020040662 (print) | LCCN 2020040663 (e-book)
ISBN 978-1-5476-0526-2 (hardcover) • ISBN 978-1-5476-0528-6 (e-book) • ISBN 978-1-5476-0527-9 (e-PDF)
Subjects: CYAC: Tree houses—Fiction. | Building—Fiction. | Leadership—
Fiction. | Determination (Personality trait)—Fiction. | Forest animals—Fiction.
Classification: LCC PZ7.1.G5513 Per 2021 (print) | LCC PZ7.1.G5513 (e-book) | DDC [Fic]—dc23
LC record available at https://lccn.loc.gov/2020040662

This art was created digitally in Photoshop, using a variety of watercolor and
dry media brushes. The display type was hand-lettered by the author.
Typeset in Copse
Book design by Leah Gilbert and Jeanette Levy
Printed in China by Leo Paper Products, Heshan, Guangdong
2 4 6 8 10 9 7 5 3 1

To find out more about our authors and books visit www.bloomsbury.com and sign up for our newsletters.

The Perfect Plan

Leah Gilbert

BLOOMSBURY
CHILDREN'S BOOKS

NEW YORK   LONDON   OXFORD   NEW DELHI   SYDNEY

Maya dreamed of having a fort.
A special, comfy, cozy place
to hide out and read,
to dream and play.

It will be the most **incredible** and *wonderful* tree fort in the world! she imagined.

She decided to make her dream come true.

She did some research,
carefully designed,

planned,

and gathered all the right supplies.

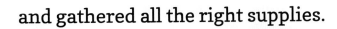

When she was sure she had thought of everything, she headed outside.

Maya hiked through the forest until she found a place that was not too sunny and not too shady, with just the right kind of fort-building trees.

Here's the perfect spot! she decided,
and went straight to work.

She started to follow her plan.
But as hard as she tried . . .

and tried . . .

and tried . . .

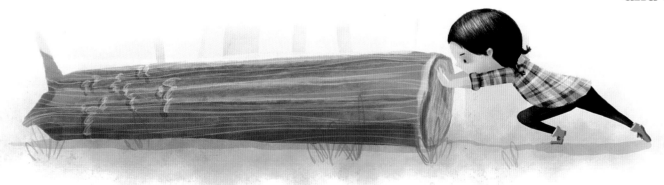

It wasn't the most incredible and wonderful fort in the world.
Actually, it wasn't looking much like a fort at all.

What if I just can't do it? she wondered.

But Maya wasn't ready to give up yet.
She had an idea.
She ran to the stream.

"I'm building the most **outstanding** and **original** tree fort in the world!" she said to the beavers. "Will you help me?"

The beavers eagerly agreed.

So, together, they cut and chopped,
split and chomped.

Soon they had a big pile of branches.

But the branches were too big and heavy
for them to move all on their own.

When Maya spied a moose peeking
through the trees, she knew the solution.

Maya and her team hurried over to the moose.
"We're building the

strongest and **sturdiest**

tree fort in the world!" she exclaimed.
"Will you help us?"

The moose enthusiastically agreed.

So, together, they heaved and tugged,

carried and lugged.

Soon all the branches
were moved.

But none of them were tall enough to lift the branches high into the trees.

Fortunately, Maya knew just which animal was a great climber!

She and her team hurried over to the bear family.
"We're building the

comfiest and coziest

tree fort in the world!" Maya exclaimed.
Will you help us?"

The bears happily agreed.

So they lifted and stacked,
built and balanced.

Soon they had created a frame.

But the branches just wouldn't stay in place.

They could use even more help!
Maya had an idea.

Maya and her team called to the birds.

"We're building the most *beautiful* and *unique* tree fort in the world!" she exclaimed. "Will you help us?"

The birds excitedly agreed.

Together, they twisted and twirled, weaved and wound.
Now all the branches were secured.

Maya and the animals studied the fort they had built together.
It was almost ready! But . . . it was still missing something.

Maya started to think. Only . . .

They were out of time.

And this was definitely not in Maya's plans.

The wind whistled and billowed.
The rain poured and pounded.
Maya cried.

"Please
don't be ruined!"

she wished with all her heart.

Maya was worried.

But maybe . . .

just maybe . . .

there was still hope.

When they arrived back at their spot,
Maya couldn't believe her eyes.
"It's **perfect!**"
she gasped.

And it was.

In fact, it was far more
than she had even imagined
it would be.